TUKTU'S
JOURNEY

Published by Arvaaq Books | www.arvaaqbooks.com

Arvaaq Books is an imprint of Inhabit Education | www.inhabiteducation.com

Inhabit Education
(Iqaluit), P.O. Box 2129, Iqaluit, Nunavut, X0A 1H0
(Toronto), 191 Eglinton Avenue East, Suite 301, Toronto, Ontario, M4P 1K1

Design and layout copyright © 2019 Inhabit Education
Text copyright © Inhabit Education
Illustrations by Ali Hinch © Inhabit Education

Printed in Canada.

ISBN: 978-0-2287-0361-7

This resource was produced as part of the QIA Benefits Fund program.

TUKTU'S JOURNEY

WRITTEN BY
Rachel Rupke

ILLUSTRATED BY
Ali Hinch

One winter morning, Tuktu wakes up early. He leaves his herd and goes for a walk. He loves the smell of the fresh morning air and the feel of the snow crunching under his hooves.

Tuktu walks and walks.

He watches the snow buntings fly above him. He sees the lemmings burrow deep in the snow.

Tuktu is ready to go back to his herd, but he has forgotten where they are!

Tuktu looks around. He wonders, **"Where are they?"**

"Hello?" he calls out. There is no answer.

"Is anyone out there?" he yells. There is no reply.

Tuktu is lost and alone. He has never been on his own before. What is he to do?

Tuktu walks on for a long time. He sees something white jumping through the snow.

"Hello?" Tuktu calls out.

An Arctic hare pops out from behind a rock. "Hello, yourself!"

Tuktu's lower lip quivers. "My name is Tuktu. I am lost. Have you seen my herd?"

"I'm Ukaliq," the hare replies. "I haven't seen your herd. But I will help you look for them!"

Ukaliq points down at Tuktu's footprints.

"Look, Tuktu!" Ukaliq says. "You make funny footprints in the snow! Let's see if we can find more caribou footprints. That could lead us to your herd!"

Ukaliq teaches Tuktu to use his eyes to look for tracks in the snow.

"I think I see something!" Tuktu exclaims. He points down at some faint tracks.

Ukaliq studies the tracks and says, "They look like caribou tracks. Let's follow them and see where they go!"

9

Tuktu and Ukaliq follow the tracks, but wind begins to blow and the tracks disappear.

"Oh, no!" Tuktu cries. "What will we do now?"

Tuktu and Ukaliq notice an Arctic fox, curled up in his den.

"Hello!" Ukaliq calls to the fox. "Sorry to bother you. My name is Ukaliq, and this is Tuktu. Tuktu has lost his herd. Have you seen a big group of caribou walking this way?"

The Arctic fox yawns, stretches, and stands up.

"I'm Tiriganiaq," he says. "I'm sorry. I haven't seen any caribou. But I will help you look for them!"

"Let's stop moving and be very quiet. If we listen carefully, we might be able to hear the herd," Tiriganiaq explains.

Tiriganiaq teaches Tuktu and Ukaliq to use their ears to listen for sounds off in the distance.

"I think I hear something!" Tuktu cries. "It's coming from over that hill!"

Ukaliq and Tiriganiaq listen carefully.

"You are right, Tuktu!" Tiriganiaq says. "There are caribou over there. Let's head in that direction!"

Tuktu, Ukaliq, and Tiriganiaq walk over the hill, following the sounds of the caribou.

When they get to the bottom of the hill, the sounds of the herd begin to fade.

"I don't hear them anymore!" Tuktu says, worried. **"Did we lose them? What will we do now?"**

Tuktu stops, sits down on the snow, and starts to cry. **"I'll never see my friends again!"**

Ukaliq and Tiriganiaq are worried for Tuktu.

Tuktu, Ukaliq, and Tiriganiaq notice a large polar bear in the distance, looking directly at them.

"Hello!" Tuktu calls out. "Can you help us?"

The polar bear lumbers over. "What seems to be the trouble?" she says.

"My name is Tuktu. These are my friends Ukaliq and Tiriganiaq. I have lost my herd. We are looking for them. Have you seen any caribou around?"

"I'm Nanuq," the polar bear says. "I haven't seen any caribou. But I can help you look for them!"

17

"I use my nose to find smells I recognize. Do you remember what your herd smells like?" Nanuq asks Tuktu.

Tuktu thinks carefully. He does remember what his herd smells like!

Tuktu, Ukaliq, Tiriganiaq, and Nanuq smell the air and the ground around them.

"I think I smell my herd!" Tuktu shouts.

Nanuq sniffs the spot Tuktu found. "Yes, I think you are right. That does smell like caribou. Let's follow that smell!"

Tuktu, Ukaliq, Tiriganiaq, and Nanuq follow the smell over the hill.

"**The smell is getting stronger!**" Tuktu calls out. The four friends pick up their pace.

"**Hmm, I'm not sure if that is the smell of caribou after all. It might be...**" Nanuq says.

Before Nanuq is able to finish his sentence, the group runs straight into...

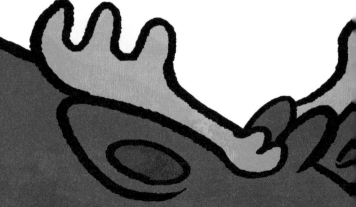

...a huge muskox!

"Hello there! What are you all doing together?"
the muskox asks.

"Hello! My name is Tuktu," Tuktu says. "These are
my new friends, Ukaliq, Tiriganiaq, and Nanuq.
I have lost my herd. We are looking for them.
Have you seen any caribou around?"

"I am Umingmak," the muskox says. "I have not
seen any caribou around here. But I will help
you look for them!"

"We have been looking all day! I don't know if we are going to be able to find my herd!" Tuktu says.

Umingmak looks at Tuktu, Ukaliq, Tiriganiaq, and Nanuq. She says, "When I need to do something difficult, I find that it is important to stay calm and not give up."

Tuktu closes his eyes and takes a deep breath. He realizes that he is surrounded by new friends, and they have all taught him helpful lessons.

Tuktu takes another big breath. "Follow me!" he calls to his new friends.

Tuktu, Ukaliq, Tiriganiaq, Nanuq, and Umingmak keep walking.
Tuktu notices some new footprints!

"Look at those marks in the snow! They are caribou
footprints!" Tuktu says to his new friends.

"Tuktu, you should smell the tracks to see if they
smell like your herd," Nanuq suggests.

Tuktu smells the footprints. "They do smell familiar!
I think this is my herd!" Tuktu says excitedly.

"Now let's stay very still and listen carefully," Tuktu whispers.

In the distance, Tuktu, Ukaliq, Tiriganiaq, Nanuq, and Umingmak can hear the sounds of caribou calling to each other.

"Do you hear that?" Tuktu exclaims. "I think my herd is close by!"

Tuktu, Ukaliq, Tiriganiaq, Nanuq, and Umingmak move quickly toward the sound.

They see something off in the distance. Could it be Tuktu's herd?

They look closer. It is!

Tuktu turns to his new friends.

"Ukaliq, thank you for teaching me to use my eyes to look for tracks in the snow.

Tiriganiaq, thank you for teaching me to use my ears to listen for my herd.

Nanuq, thank you for teaching me to use my nose to smell for the scent of my herd.

Umingmak, thank you for teaching me to never give up.

Without the four of you, I never would have found my herd!"

Tuktu takes one more look at his new friends. He gives them a smile, turns, and runs toward his herd.

Tuktu knows he is a lucky caribou. He has found his herd, and he has four new friends!

33

Act out the story!

Puppets have been created for each of the characters in this story.

As you read this story with children, encourage them to act out the story using the puppets. Once children are familiar with the story, they can use the puppets to retell the main storyline independently. Children can also be encouraged to make up their own stories about the puppet characters.

TUKTU

Inuktitut for "caribou"

pronounced
took-too

UKALIQ

Inuktitut for "Arctic hare"

pronounced
oo-kah-leek

TIRIGANIAQ

Inuktitut for "Arctic fox"

pronounced
tee-ree-gah-nee-ack

NANUQ

Inuktitut for "polar bear"

pronounced
nah-nook

36

UMINGMAK

Inuktitut for "muskox"

pronounced
oo-ming-mack

ARVAAQ
BOOKS